MISSION
CONTAMINATION

Stories From Scotland

Edited By Brixie Payne

First published in Great Britain in 2019 by:

 Young**Writers**® — Est. 1991 —

Young Writers
Remus House
Coltsfoot Drive
Peterborough
PE2 9BF
Telephone: 01733 890066
Website: www.youngwriters.co.uk

FOREWORD

Young Writers was created in 1991 with the express purpose of promoting and encouraging creative writing. Each competition we create is tailored to the relevant age group, hopefully giving each student the inspiration and incentive to create their own piece of work, whether it's a poem, mini saga or a short story. We truly believe that seeing their work in print gives students a sense of achievement and pride in their work and themselves.

Our Survival Sagas series aimed to challenge both the young writers' creativity and their survival skills! One of the biggest challenges, aside from dodging diseased hordes and avoiding the contagion, was to create a story with a beginning, middle and end in just 100 words!

Inspired by the theme of contamination, whether from a natural mutation, a chemical attack or a man-made experiment gone wrong, their mission was to craft tales of fear and redemption, new beginnings and struggles of survival against the odds. As you will discover, these students rose to the challenge magnificently and we can declare *Mission Contamination* a success.

The mini sagas in this collection are sure to set your pulses racing and leave you wondering with each turn of the page: are these writers born survivors?

CONTENTS

Estella Adeline Ancia McNeill Conner (14)	60
Rachel Quinn (12)	61
Juliet Hobson (13)	62
Rachel Thompson (12)	63
Emilie Turner (12)	64
Carla Crawford (13)	65
Joshua Freel (12)	66
Calum Gordon (12)	67
Heather Blair (13)	68
Aimee Paterson-Caddell (14)	69
Mathieu J Terry (13)	70
Josh Douglas Hill (12)	71
Ryan Masterman (13)	72
Sarah Convery (12)	73
Kris Ferguson (12)	74
Callan McKee (13)	75
Anya Clare Milligan (12)	76
Archie Scollin (12)	77
Brodie Donaldson (12)	78
Scarlett Macnamara (12)	79
Keziah Elizabeth Reid (12)	80
Lauren Turner (13)	81
Lee Adams (13)	82
Victoria Eve Murdoch (13)	83
Robbie Woods (12)	84
Ellise Fitzgerald (14)	85
Emma McLarty (12)	86
Laurie Smith (12)	87
John Wilson (12)	88
Caera Murray (12)	89
Ruby Wilson (12)	90
James Harrison (12)	91
Mia Caldwell Stevenson (12)	92

Levenmouth Academy, Buckhaven

Logan Peden (12)	93
Leah Nisbet (14)	94
Alyx Winn (12)	95
Emma Louise Roberts (15)	96
Holly Tracy Wilson (17)	97
Aymen Rao Rizwan (13)	98

Joseph Wilson (12)	99
Jason Yule (13)	100
Declan Ferrier (12)	101
Hollie Elizabeth Glenn McCulloch (12)	102
Jaimie Ann Thomson Walters (14)	103
Jasmin Scarlett (13)	104
Tyler Wilson	105
Dylan Keddie (13)	106

McLaren High School, Callander

Scott Stewart (13)	107
Tom McCulloch (13)	108
Hannah Docherty (13)	109
Robert Tweedie	110
Benjamin Snow (13)	111
Camryn Taylor Reynolds (12)	112

Stewarton Academy, Stewarton

Codie McGowan (12)	113
Lara Haine (13)	114
Molly McDade (14)	115
May McLaughlin (14)	116
Teagan Neish (15)	117
Ellie Anderson (14)	118
Johanna-Ellie Robertson (14)	119
Louise Macaulay (13)	120
Blake Hannah (14)	121
Madeline Esther McIlreavy (14)	122
Jamie Mitchell (14)	123
Christopher Lennon (14)	124
Emily Smith (14)	125
Alexander Caulfield (14)	126
Catriona Muir (12)	127
Faris Marshall (14)	128
Rebecca Smith (14)	129
Max McCaughran (13)	130
Jane Docherty McDowell (15)	131
Adam Nadeem (15)	132
Emma Nimmo (14)	133
Peter A Millar (12)	134

Niamh Russell (12)   135
Malcolm Millar (12)   136
Rhuaridh Longstaff (12)   137
Nathan Lamont McDowell (12)   138
Zara Elizabeth Conroy-   139
Rodger (14)
Eilidh Allan (14)   140
Josslyn Fletcher (14)   141
Kyle Maitland (12)   142
Cara Moffat (12)   143

Webster's High School, Kirriemuir

Isla Webb (12)   144
Cassandra Calder (16)   145
Cora East   146
Rory Fyles (13)   147
Alix Burness (15)   148
Ellie Craib (12)   149
Anna Goubet (14)   150

THE MINI SAGAS

No Remorse

He didn't feel any remorse for the infected. After all, his job was to eliminate them, not cure them. Phantom crouched on the roof, flanked by Scorch and Fury as he watched some of the infected stagger on by, whilst sharpening his scythes for the upcoming battle.

"Do we really have to?" asked Scorch, more out of concern for her fellow teammates than pity.

"We know our mission," Fury answered, robotically. "Nothing leaves here alive!"

Phantom remained silent. After a while, he stood up. "It's time," he said. "Deploy."

Then they ambushed the infected with fire, bullets and blades.

Alex McKenzie (16)

Annan Academy, Annan

Zombie Zania

"The moment has come!" said the mad scientist. "Time to unleash the virus!"

At that moment, virus canisters were being loaded onto some rockets and blasted off to infect the unsuspecting innocent citizens of the world! Once the rockets crashed in countries such as Spain, Portugal, Scotland and England, it let off a stinky smell. Once breathed in, it changes that person into a zombie. Millions of people were infected with only a few survivors, leading to the horrific end of the world as we know it. Soon, the mad scientist was made the extreme, ruthless ruler of Zombie Zania.

Scott Irving (12)
Annan Academy, Annan

The Great Plague

Homes were abandoned. Bodies flooded streets and even I began to get signs of an infection. Let me tell you how the world ended. It was Friday, I think, when scientists in Sicily revived the plague to research but it infected them and more people died. The world was ending with Europe at the centre. It was chaos. People set homes on fire to purify the demonic world. Medical professionals were scrutinised for not having the cure.
On Saturday, a plague doctor came from America. He too couldn't remain pure and this is the story of how the world ended.

Neil Alexander (13)
Annan Academy, Annan

Possessed

She struggled to breathe, her breaths getting shorter. Could it be poison? She was urged towards a purple light at the end of the corridor. It all went black. When she awoke, her vision was blurred... and colours, colours all around. Where was she? How did she get there? The buzzing all around her made it difficult to think. Was she hallucinating? She felt like she was being controlled as she got to her feet. She heard footsteps. She turned around to see a strange figure walking towards her. She was drawn to it. It could control her every move...

Eve Campbell (12)
Annan Academy, Annan

Acid

Have you ever looked up at the sky and wondered what was behind those glistening stars? Aliens? A parallel universe? Well, in that parallel universe, the entirety of mankind are dying. As I'm writing this, I can see a grey sky full of clouds, full of... well, rain, but rain can't do anything, only make you damp, right? Well, their rain is as toxic as acid and will burn you to a crisp, on the spot. There are no houses, no towns, no schools, only death and destruction. There is almost no human existence whatsoever. Well, goodnight.

Gabriella Nolan (12)
Annan Academy, Annan

No Escape

Jessica unlocked the door, she could hear a loud thumping. She was ready to shoot anybody infected with the virus. The noise got louder. Then this *thing* burst through the wall. It was hideous, it seemed to have grown a third arm but it was three times the size of its normal one. It was like a fleshy mass with claws and one giant red eye staring at her. She opened fire directly at the eye. She noticed how the flesh spread like a virus down its body. The creature fell to one knee. But Jessica knew it wasn't over.

Harley Bruton (12)

Annan Academy, Annan

My Evil Pet And I

We finally emerged from the underground bunker. It was dark and foggy, but there were still no clues how my pet turned evil. It was one night where it all happened. I was sleeping and could hear a rattling noise in his cage. I turned around and my hamster was ten times bigger with glowing red eyes. I had no chance of escaping.

I must have been bitten and put to sleep because I don't remember going down to a basement. All I saw was me lying on a metal bed and beaming red eyes, staring at me creepily.

Abigail Mia Glen (14)

Annan Academy, Annan

It's Spreading

It had been years since I had been injected with the potion. But only now had I noticed the effects. My arm where I had been injected was turning a murky brown. I began to panic as it crept up my shoulder. Soon, my whole arm was the colour of a swamp. I ran onto the street, looking for help but no one would come near me as it crawled up my neck. I caught my reflection in a window. It was just my head left. Soon, it was covering my face. I had one word in my mind. *Kill!*

Tait Render (12)
Annan Academy, Annan

The Cloud

We finally emerged from the underground bunker. The city was destroyed and there was a dark red cloud that was killing the people of Japan. When we got out, we had to hide. We went to a shed that was still standing. After that, we had to find food and water. Olabo was the place to go. When they got there, they locked up. They had food and water but then the red cloud emerged out of the vents and then... They ran as fast as they could but couldn't escape the cloud!

Jack Hilton (12)

Annan Academy, Annan

The Virus

It was a great day until every computer and TV stopped working. The first week without the computers and TVs was fine. Until people started breaking into other people's houses and people started getting killed. Then cars stopped working. Money stopped getting made. The world was falling apart. We didn't know how much we needed technology and people didn't know how to act. The world was going to end very soon and it was all because of technology. Then everybody's computers started sparking. They were going to explode. It was almost like they were synchronised. Then *bang!*

Dylan Rose (12)
Braeview Academy, Dundee

No Survivors

"What's that noise?" Sarah said to her husband. Her husband turned around slowly. Steven's face was skinless and he had a terrifying grin on his face. Sarah loudly screamed and ran out her house with only her pyjamas on. Sarah screamed again after seeing all her neighbours with no skin on their faces. They ran to her.

Sarah ran into the lake, without knowing that the water was giving everyone the infection. Her hands moved towards her face without her moving them, and she ripped the skin off her face. No survivors were left in the infected town.

Finlay Reid (12)
Braeview Academy, Dundee

Uninstalled

I stayed late in a computer science room when I heard a mysterious whistle next door. I wanted to check when I tripped over multiple memory cards. I fell downstairs, face planting each step I hit. I tried stopping but I slid on a CD, falling over the bannister, hitting the floor.

I woke up, stunned, to a girl in a white dress. I said, "What are you doing?"

She reverted her whole head 180 degrees, looking sharply into my eyes with her black eyes. I looked over to the screen in front of her. It said "Uninstall world... processing..."

Rustams Malisevs (12)

Braeview Academy, Dundee

Lovers

Isaac pointed the gun at his struggling lover. He loved her to bits; now he had to kill her due to that disease that was slowly but definitely making her insane, eating at her brain until she became so violent she would kill others. Her veins were black. Suddenly, a loud clang sounded off the walls and Vanessa was trying to get to her feet. She was stopped by the handcuffs that held her to the radiator.

"Isaac, now. Please." Vanessa's eyes were clear of any insanity that had previously been there. He closed his eyes then pulled the trigger.

Ellie Elizabeth Gibson (13)

Braeview Academy, Dundee

Patient Zero

We were travelling in an APC transporting a patient infected with a new pathogen. We were told nothing, ordered just to take it for testing. We weren't told about any dangers or what it would do to us if it escaped.

Our driver was distracted and as we turned the corner, we crashed and flipped. We crawled out of the flaming wreckage, as did the patient. He looked normal apart from the boils on his chest. We readied our rifles, itching to pull the triggers. My second in command walked forward to try and apprehend it.

We were too late...

Callan Liddell (13)

Braeview Academy, Dundee

Home Planet

"3075 hurry up. We need to go now!"

I can't believe it. I'm going to see Earth. It was terrible what happened to it but apparently, it's safe now. I go aboard the spacecraft. Honestly though, I never thought I'd ever get a chance to see such a big part of the human race's history.

"We are now landing on Earth."

I am so excited but when I get off the spacecraft I am shocked. There is nothing; just old runes and the stench of rotting flesh. I look around me and all I see are bones and bodies.

Hannah McFee (12)

Braeview Academy, Dundee

They're Here

I woke up to the blood-curdling sound of screaming, shouting and strange voices.
"Stand back and get behind the fence."
I looked outside my window to see these inhuman things eating people. They're here. A couple of months ago, an outbreak of a virus started so our city was prepared. But clearly not enough, because it's getting closer and closer. Until it's in the house, more than one. I can't move, there's nowhere to go. It's getting closer. I try to run but it's too late. It's got me.

Chloe Weldon (13)
Braeview Academy, Dundee

Simon's Story

I am injected with fluid that seems to drown my physical features. My veins ooze with foamy acidic fluid, continuing to break down my existence. Somehow I doze, but I am still able to connect with my feelings. Why am I facing such punishment? Why? Shouldn't I be dead by now? This is too unreal!

Seeing an armed man outside, I realise that I am under captivity. Looking around, I can make out a card saying 'get well soon'. The man walks towards me, wearing a one-piece suit, holding a needle. I realise this is the instrument of my death.

Amy Stewart (14)
Braeview Academy, Dundee

Bad Rash

The rash was spreading, killing everyone. No one knows what started it, but everyone who has it has died. We have got scientists looking at some bodies to see what has caused it. If the scientists don't find out what happened, they will lose their jobs and will get shot.

The government probably knows but they're not telling us because they don't want us to get scared. We will solve this, with or without the government telling us or helping us. The president has told everyone not to worry. But we know he can't be trusted.

Ben Russell (12)
Braeview Academy, Dundee

The Virus

The town's silent; well, the majority of it. I mean, some nights I hear people growling in pain as their bodies get less and less human-like - missing limbs, no nose or ears, things like that. Nobody knows what it is or how it's caused. But what we do know is that once you start experiencing the symptoms, it's only a matter of time before you become another one of this horrendous virus' victims. I mean I wouldn't mind dying, rather be dead than living in this hellhole that was once my safe, quiet town.

Kelly Roy (13)
Braeview Academy, Dundee

Sister

It's been spreading for days now. People say it can cause bad, bad illnesses, some say even death. I do not want me and my family to catch this disease. My friend... Phone rings... oh no, my sister has just caught the disease. I must go to the hospital.

"Your sister is in very good hands, but her health is very bad."

What if she dies? She's my only sister. She can't die. I can't let her die.

I run into my sister's hospital room. "Wake up. Please wake up!"

Kenzie Parnell (12)
Braeview Academy, Dundee

Last One Left

Nobody knew what was happening, but everyone knew something was wrong. My heart was racing, my head was spinning. Then suddenly... a raindrop fell, and instantly I felt calm. The grass surrounding me was turning grey. Delusional? I wish. My eyes were burning. All I could hear were screams and cries. Then it all went silent, and everyone dropped to the ground. Was I the only one alive? I partly wished I wasn't. Day by day, I was rotting away, like what had happened to the rest and I couldn't do anything about it.

Tegan Williamson
Braeview Academy, Dundee

The End

I woke up with a burning sensation throughout my body. It was the virus I had injected in my leg, thinking it might heal my cancer. I thought surely the burning feeling would go away soon. The pain just escalated into the feeling of death. I know that sounds a little over dramatic but my skin was changing into the way a dead body would. I started to feel nothing, then that's when it happened. The hunger started to take over and it was all I could think of. I changed others with a bite and was officially Patient Zero.

Shannon Sandra Taylor (13)
Braeview Academy, Dundee

The Lump

I wake with a start, my hair sticking up with sweat, while hearing my heart in my head, feeling a weird sensation in my leg. Then I look down. There is a lump and it's moving! I try to scream but I have no voice. I don't know what to do. Then I look around. My surroundings are unknown, it's dark and damp and I'm all alone. Where am I? What day is it? How long have I been here? What is wrong with me? I look down at my leg. It's back to normal but now there's something else...

Makayla Irene Walker (13)
Braeview Academy, Dundee

Patient C

"Tested patient C is unaccounted for..." was the last thing we heard. If only we knew why the patient went by 'C', things would maybe be different now.

After that day everything was silent. Months had gone by and there was hardly anyone left. I was in silence when I heard a bang on the door. By this time the house was in darkness and I was all alone... well, at least I thought I was. I felt an excruciating pain in my leg. I looked down and let out a scream. I realised I was now one of them.

Alyssa Dowdles (13)

Braeview Academy, Dundee

The Black Death

It had been weeks since I felt okay. My mum had just died from an unknown disease and I was scared I was getting it too. The doctors had given me medicine but I continued to vomit and scratch like mad. My skin had become black but my face was white and I couldn't stop being sick. My dad had just started having the same symptoms me and mum had and I was extremely worried. I started vomiting blood and the medicine wasn't helping. My dad took me to the hospital but it was too late. My heart stopped.

Louise Reid (13)
Braeview Academy, Dundee

The Experiment

The last drop went into the test tube. *Bang!* The test tube exploded and the room was filled with thick black smoke. Within that smoke was a pair of red beady eyes. Then the monster appeared. It was seven foot tall with big sharp teeth and red spines down its back. It had hair like a wolf. It turned around and smashed through the wall with insane rage. Then I heard people screaming from outside the building. I looked outside and the hairy monster was running down the road, growling in insane rage.

Joshua James Elsom (12)
Braeview Academy, Dundee

Crazy Virus

Suddenly, the lights went out. There were screams, shouts. The lights went on. The city was contaminated. Some people had started to have heart attacks. Some had turned green. People had to escape. People ran. About 167 people made it out alive but there was no way to save people from the contamination. Scientists tried to find a cure but they didn't find one. All the city was contaminated. There was a loud storm. They heard yells. The zombies found the people and charged. There were no survivors.

Lucas Ross Paterson (12)
Braeview Academy, Dundee

The Rash

The rash was spreading and hurting lots of people. People were dying one by one. Nearly everybody was affected by the rash apart from three people called Fred, Finlay, and Jonny. The three were confused when they heard about the rash. Jonny was so scared. He wanted to go to the hospital because he thought he was going to die. But one week later, Jonny died a slow and painful death. The others buried him in the back garden so they could remember him. Fred was so sad because Jonny was his best friend.

Robbie Allan Gibb (13)

Braeview Academy, Dundee

Contaminated

It is the year 2074 and the place where I lived (Bolton) was gone. A deadly virus had spread through England in the year 2068. I'm one of the last 56 alive that we know of. Everyone else is either dead or a zombie.

My role in survival is to be on lookout. But one night, something terrible happens. I must have fallen asleep because when I wake up, I hear screaming coming from the camp. I look in one of the tents and what I see is horrifying. Everyone has been contaminated. I am alone.

Josh Reekie (14)
Braeview Academy, Dundee

The Flashback

Just after the needle he had flashbacks. He had a disease that if he went to sleep he would sleep, and if he wouldn't get to sleep he would stay up the whole night. When that happened an old lady would appear in his room and would sing a song. If he did go to sleep, then he wouldn't wake up until someone died. One night, no one died and his family buried him in his back garden. He woke up and realised that he was not dreaming - he was buried under the ground for the second time!

Darci Rhynd (12)
Braeview Academy, Dundee

Zombie Apocalypse

I was walking home from school when I saw everyone running, telling me to get inside. I was confused so I just kept walking. But then I saw a figure walking very slowly towards me saying, "Brains! Brains! I want brains!" I noticed it was a zombie!
I ran as fast as I could and eventually made it to my house. I walked into the living room, when I saw my mum saying that there were zombies and that we had to go. I ran and packed my things and went to my mum's car.

Madison Lee Digan
Braeview Academy, Dundee

The Z-Virus

I felt it, I mean the needle, and it didn't hurt.
C'mon, the doctor was trustworthy. Yet, when I
was talking to him he was nice but I knew he was
hiding something.

Of course it was that he was making me a super-
soldier. Anyway, I opened my eyes, looked up and
saw it - the canister. It said 'Z-Virus'.

It began; the pain, ah, the pain. I was in agony and
I changed. I couldn't think straight. The only word
in my head at the time was 'hunger'.

Bailey James Edwards (14)
Braeview Academy, Dundee

Buried Alive!

I can feel it... slowly approaching. The knife going through my chest slow and sharp. All of a sudden it is dark, cold and wet. It feels like something caving into my chest slowly but painfully.

A few hours pass by - still no clue where I am or why I'm there. I can hear people so I shout but they can't hear me... I start to panic. I can barely move. I start to get really tense and shaky. I can't feel anything except this strange liquid pouring out of me...

Teigan Williams (14)
Braeview Academy, Dundee

The Injection

I can feel it... the pinch of the injection... the surge of the fluid gushing down my left arm... Then the burning started... first in my arm, then all the way down to my toes, spreading all through my skull... Then everything went numb...

That was the last thing I'd ever felt... That was my last day of living... because... now... I am a 'zombie' and I eat people... I can't help it of course... It's... well, in my nature I guess...

Tiegan McIntyre (14)
Braeview Academy, Dundee

In The Lab

I walked into work. It looked fine. It was 6.15 in the morning. It was silent, too silent. I got scared. The door slammed shut. I jumped. I walked back. I knocked over a container of chemical Z. Something came out of the ground - it was a hand. Then it was a-another, another hand. Then it was a head. Then it was the whole body. I screamed. No one could hear me scream. I tried to run but the hand grabbed me and started to pull me back in.

Nicole Dailly (12)
Braeview Academy, Dundee

The Sun

How am I going to last these last few days? The sun is so deadly, I feel like giving up. I can't bear this anymore; I just want a normal life. If only the sun was the same again so I can go to the beach again and be with my mum and brother again. I miss them so much. Maybe I should just look at the sun. But what if there is hope? I highly doubt. Reconsidering, I lie down and take my fold off...

Aimee Mary Millar (12)
Braeview Academy, Dundee

The Virus

It all started on a normal day in 2017. Nobody suspected a thing. There was nothing wrong. Then it happened - Vauxhall Zafiras started to set on fire and blow up. People started dying with the blasts. Nobody knew what was causing the cars to explode. Eventually, someone took their car to a scientist and they found out that the cars had a virus. They found out too late. The virus had spread...

Aaron Simpson (12)
Braeview Academy, Dundee

Teatime

The rash was spreading through the city and rapidly killing people. It all started with a virus in the city. It was in a drink of Coke in the shop and was now spreading throughout the city. There are only a couple of survivors and now they will have to hide until the apocalypse is over. You don't want to get the virus because if you do, you will be a zombie and eat people for tea.

Brandon Soutar (12)
Braeview Academy, Dundee

Death Wish

I regain consciousness to find I'm strapped to a hard steel bed and can't move. I hear someone shuffling towards me and see a flash of a white coat. There's an odd smell in the air, almost like rotten flesh. A shadow looms over me then teeth tear into my neck and I know I'm going to die.

Kaitlyn Allan
Braeview Academy, Dundee

The Terrible Events Of The Supermarket

Finally emerging from the underground bunker, we found everything calm and normal. We quickly switched the wireless on to check for an 'all clear' but there were just warnings about contamination in a reservoir. We started to run out of food quickly because Mum was pregnant. I had to keep a look out for zombies or gas clouds to keep us all safe. I decided to run to the supermarket which was minutes away. I walked in and bought supplies, then handed over the change to a... zombie! He bit me and I fell. I knew it was all over...

Skye Sneddon (12)
Grangemouth High School, Grangemouth

Rampage

The rash was spreading, pulsing. My entire body was in pain. I couldn't move a single limb. My bed was practically a prison cell. Over time, I felt as if my mind was being turned to mush until... I snapped. I shot out of bed and started trashing everything. My room turned into a war zone; TVs were cracked, bulbs were smashed, windows were completely destroyed and when my mind returned from its rampage, all I could focus on was one thing - my dog, Buster. He was just lying there completely drenched in his dark, warm blood.

Kai Bowman (12)
Grangemouth High School, Grangemouth

It's Torture

I've got it... Some people think I'm joking around but I'm not. How can I be? The only people who have it are dead... It takes over your whole body. First, you start to catch a fever so hot you feel like your stomach is on fire. Then it goes dark, your eyes turn black. Everything goes dark. You see nothing! There is no cure because it's not very common. With the sharp, stabbing pain and the lack of air, I feel electric shocks from the tips of my fingers, into my brain. It's torture.

Robyn Vause (12)
Grangemouth High School, Grangemouth

Operation Z

Where is it? Area 51 - the great fortress. No more!
Infested with these things we call 'mutants'. Two
patients had escaped. The military were called in.
They walled off the fortress. There were no
survivors. We had to kill everything in there. It was
time for Team Delta to show them who was really
boss of Area 51. We didn't know if we would come
out alive. We all had extended riot shields with
reinforced street plates and the best pistols for the
job. This would be my toughest job yet...

Rowan Stewart (12)
Grangemouth High School, Grangemouth

Monster Lab

I'm starting to feel really ill; I don't know why. I am throwing up a lot and the strangest thing is, my skin has started to become green. I just want to be cured of this illness. It's been going on for three days now.

The next day... It's all becoming clearer now. About four days ago, I was in the lab and just as I was leaving I knocked over a test tube. It spilt over me. I think the lab workers are planning to wipe out the human race with zombies. Am I one of them?

Amy Fegan (12)
Grangemouth High School, Grangemouth

Disappear

The last drop fell from the test tube. It was the end. They were going to make me drink it. Would I come out alive? I had to run for it, but how? The crazy scientist turned around to open the door. Who was that? I sat up and ran at the scientist. *Boom!* Was he okay? I ran past the crazy scientist into the cold winter weather. I saw the scientist getting up. I don't think he saw me. I heard him say in his deep voice, "Subject A has disappeared. Get Subject B in!"

Roksana Rybarczyk (12)
Grangemouth High School, Grangemouth

New York Gone

A big area of New York City was poisoned by a
massive nuclear bomb that blew up on December
30th, 1980. We need a lot of help. People who
weren't protected turned into a weird type of
zombie! Their faces were all burned but they
survived the nuclear blast somehow... These
'things' are attracted to my food and water. And
I'm stuck out here. The army's no use! These
creatures are breaking down my door. Aaah... my
face, it burns, it burns. God help me!

Aedan Stuart Couser (12)
Grangemouth High School, Grangemouth

Contaminated Cloud

The giant contaminated cloud eventually rose up into the sky. I hoped that the experiment worked! The experiment was for the cloud to rain over the huge forest to see if the plants could grow faster. But if the chemicals used in the cloud came into contact with humans, it would not end smoothly. I noticed that someone was walking through the forest. This couldn't be happening! Who was that? What if they get contaminated? What would happen? Would it spread?

Eve Hamilton
Grangemouth High School, Grangemouth

Trapped

There were vines everywhere. The cold was nipping at my fingertips. It was dark and I was lonely. I decided I would need to do something soon or I would just start to rot away in this corner of an abandoned classroom. I stood up and I popped my head out of the door, but all I could see was the cloudy, glossy puddle of the contaminated glue stuff. And then I heard it...

Summer Noë (12)
Grangemouth High School, Grangemouth

The Apocalypse

It was a massacre. The apocalypse has begun.
"Our lazy government won't lift a finger!" bellowed Fred.
The government were doing absolutely nothing to stop this happening. Zombies around every corner, more by the minute.
"I'm fixing this," muttered Fred.
This scientist was about to attempt the impossible... to end the apocalypse. From dawn until dusk, Fred worked tirelessly to create an antidote for the undead, each result more horrific than before.
After ten sleepless nights, he'd finally done it! All he needed was his plan to work. His face glistened with sweat. Fred activated the machine. Goodbye forever, apocalypse.

Jaydon Fisher (12)
Largs Academy, Largs

The Lie, Death And Cure

"The infection's a lie!" an old scientist yelled, but no one believed him...

They believed he was infected. They shunned him, saying his mutated DNA was the reason he was infected. Day after day, people were turned away, never to return. They say, "If it isn't normal, they're infected." Everyone believed them.

No research was done on the cure, people were just sent to the unknown abyss. Every day the town decreased, from 50 to 2...

If we stay, we'll starve. If we leave, we'll be infected. Do we listen to them or find what will save us? The cure...

Scarlet Barton-Holtz (13)

Largs Academy, Largs

Virus Gone Viral

The virus was spreading.

It started in the fingers and then travelled all around the body. From one touch of a phone, iPad, computer and so on, you'd die. No one knew that you caught it by touching a device. Scientists and engineers had been trying to figure out how it came from electronic devices ever since they discovered it. But they'd got nowhere.

On the 5th of April 2019, the virus started spreading. Everyone and anyone touching an electronic device would most likely die within 24 hours of catching this mysterious, untreatable, deadly virus. It's a virus gone viral.

Keir Henderson (12)

Largs Academy, Largs

Sausage Roll Disaster

Sitting in his lab, Scientist Jimmy was thinking about how to defeat the giant sausage rolls attacking the world! Ever since last week, humongous sausage rolls have been destroying all the humans, so it has to be sorted! Within two days, hundreds of humans have died due to these beasts! Yesterday, Scientist Jimmy invented a weapon to kill them with called The Ketchupinator. Watch Jimmy pull the trigger. You'll see ketchup squirt into the beast's mouths and kill him! Did this ingenious contraption work? Yes! Nearly all the sausage rolls have been killed and thrown out of the world!

Isla Archbold (12)

Largs Academy, Largs

No One Left

The knobbly rash was spreading round the school as fast as the speed of light. Soon the school was completely deserted. Even the teachers had contracted this loathsome, lethal disease out of nowhere. The quick-spreading disease had completely wiped out the school. Everyone was slowly dying. People all over the world were now catching it. The number of the human population was rapidly decreasing by millions. It had now been six months and the human race had almost fully been defeated. There was no food left. No crops, no nothing. Everyone knew they wouldn't last even one more week.

Georgia Kirkwood (12)
Largs Academy, Largs

No Escape, No Rescue

There was no way out. Jayden slammed the door, frustratedly.

"The key, where is it?" She was getting desperate. Jayden thought that everyone had to have died, just dropping like flies. There was no cure. No chance of rescue; they were all doomed. Although, Jayden was known to be very determined and she would not give up, no matter what lay ahead. She tried again and again. The flames spread across the room. She tried again and burst through. She was right, everyone had died. Clutching her heart, she just lay there and gave up. The disease had killed everyone.

Jordan John Docherty (12)
Largs Academy, Largs

Nowhere Is Safe

We finally emerged from the bunker, hoping the cannibals had gone. They'd taken everyone and everything. Nowhere's safe. There were six people with us, now only four, plus me - the scientist, the doctor, the hunter, the teacher and me. We started walking, trying to find food. There were no signs of civilisation. We could hear them running about, looking, waiting for people. We could see the lab where we needed to go, there was a cure that could help wipe out the cannibals. There were some at the side of the building. We started running. They emerged, running, screaming.

Laila Campbell Stevenson (12)
Largs Academy, Largs

The Silence Of New York

We finally emerged from the underground bunker. The disease had spread quickly. New York was silent. It was impossible to develop a cure. But we needed to, quickly. Corpses lay everywhere. That's when I realised why they wanted to keep us in the bunkers. But we were starving and dehydrated. The best option was to wait for someone or something. But silence was the only sound. Our future was not looking so good. The scientists that were left had investigated and found that it was DNA mutation. That didn't change anything. There was still no hope or cure for humanity.

Maria McKechnie (12)
Largs Academy, Largs

Experimental

It was the year 2097. A mad scientist danced and hopped around his dark underground bunker. In front of him stood three test subjects, each of different ages. Beside him, the sacred potion to turn humans to animals. He grabbed the potion and gave the test subjects a taste. They started to transform, but not into animals. Their heads started to jitter, followed by their arms and legs and, finally, they were transformed. Their eyes were bright yellow and they all had big grinning smiles. They broke the glass they were caged in and walked slowly, edging towards the scientist.

Amy Wilson (12)
Largs Academy, Largs

Outbreak

The doctor studied the vial, searching for proof that a cure was possible but before he could examine it further, the code red alarm went off and he heard screeching in the distance. He knew impending doom approached him. The infected were basically zombies but with the same abilities as the previous host, such as running, jumping and climbing. They were predators and their prey was humanity. They had nearly wiped out most of humanity at this point. The people left were killing each other for the limited resources left. But everyone on this planet knew mankind was doomed.

Aidan Meechan (13)

Largs Academy, Largs

Eco Gone Lethal

Humanity is definitely ending, but the worst part is it's all my fault. When I ingeniously invented a contraption to stop pollution, never did I think it would poison everyone. That really wasn't my original plan. When I travelled to the G8 Summit to unveil my new invention, it suddenly released gas into the atmosphere. All the world leaders and I managed to swiftly escape into an underground bunker. Unfortunately, the poisonous gas is now spreading to the rest of the world and our food is running short. We need to form a plan before the human race is destroyed.

Katie Trotter (13)

Largs Academy, Largs

The Martians

Nothing could stop them, the Martians. They came suddenly, bringing a disease which was harmless to them, yet fatal to us. All the streets seemed deserted, no one was left. Strangely, I was immune to this but instead of being delighted I was traumatised. Was this the end? I was completely alone and no one could save me. Silently, I sat trembling on the armchair that was my dad's favourite, tears streaming down my face. All hope was lost, until I saw a young boy outside my window, pacing the street, wearing a worried expression. Maybe there were other survivors...

Estella Adeline Ancia McNeill Conner (14)
Largs Academy, Largs

Goodbye

Nobody knows where they came from. Nobody knows when they will leave the Earth. They wiped out everyone, except the ones who hid. And they'll be hiding for much longer if they want to survive the attacks. The aliens have taken over all places on Earth where humans used to live. The people who did hide only have limited resources and they're running out. Some of them need to venture out and try to smuggle resources for the remaining population. Nobody wants to go because they will almost instantly get caught. They need to decide who needs to venture out.

Rachel Quinn (12)
Largs Academy, Largs

Liberator

I sit alone in the dark bunker which has become home in the past months. I can't sleep. They say we're nearly there, we have nearly completed Liberator, the spaceship which will take us to galaxies unknown. Mankind's only hope after the apocalypse. I hate that gas, the gas which caused all of this. One breath and the friendliest of people will turn into murderers, slaying anything near them. It was made to win wars but instead spread like a deadly, invisible wildfire across the world. Only five percent of life remains. All we can do now is escape.

Juliet Hobson (13)
Largs Academy, Largs

Being Brave

"It's okay boy, it's me," growled the shadow.
The boy felt scared as he entered the cave. The shadow kept calling him. The boy didn't know what it was, but then he saw a dark and creepy shadow. He glared into the shadow's eyes and saw nothing but evil in them. Everyone was gone. The boy had the cure, ready for the shadow to come out and attack him.

"I'm not afraid of you," the boy shouted, as his voice echoed around the cave. The shadow came running at him. The boy stabbed the cure into him. They were saved.

Rachel Thompson (12)

Largs Academy, Largs

Microbes From Mars

"Spacecraft 297 lands on Mars, 2027," states Mr McNulty from an old newspaper from 367 years ago. Eddie Malcoff is reading whilst standing outside a metal room in NYC with an infected spacecraft inside. Anyone who enters, trying to solve the problem, dies. Eddie is trying to find a way to get this infection, called Nomadexia, off spacecraft 297.

Eddie Malcoff and Harold Jones have mixed an antidote and are now suiting up to go and stop this disease from killing any more people. Harold and Eddie reach spacecraft 297 and destroy it. Eddie dies.

Emilie Turner (12)
Largs Academy, Largs

Alone

You can't run from it, no matter how hard you try. It's like a snake that crushes your throat until you can't breathe. It's like an invisible bullet that goes directly through your heart and leaves you in pain until you fall down dead. Has the world really come to this? We are helpless rats in a cage. People are living in fear, too scared to enter the houses of people we've known for years because it's every man for himself. Every day this voice in your head always saying, *this is it... this is the end... you're alone.*

Carla Crawford (13)
Largs Academy, Largs

The Last Few

The human race has contracted a disease. This mass-killing infection has almost wiped out the whole world. All because of a miscount when doing a genetic engineering test to exterminate a deadly gas. So the government put a dome over the town, then they came looking for a cure that didn't exist. Apparently, there is one person outside who is immune to the infection. He contacted us saying that he is taking a blood sample from himself and transferring it into the infected. It didn't seem to be working apart from a mother and daughter in Texas...

Joshua Freel (12)

Largs Academy, Largs

Sketchy Scientist

Bob the scientist accidentally knocked over a test tube. When he was cleaning up, the harmful chemicals got on his skin, giving him an unbearable rash. It was spreading like the flu, from one person to the next. The scientists tried frantically to find a cure, but they were slowly dying. If they did not come up with something fast, they would be a thing of the past. They were becoming weaker by the minute. They would have no hope. One of the scientist's hands slipped and the two liquids mixed. It's all or nothing. Would they find a cure?

Calum Gordon (12)
Largs Academy, Largs

Trees Are Gone

The human race is going to end. Trees are all gone. Families say bye to their loved ones. Time's running out. Unless a tree grows with the necessary chemicals, fast. Scientists are working as hard as possible to find the solution. They have tried everything, nothing has worked - from plant grower to mixing elements together. We are running out of time. Over 3.9 billion people have died. The last people to survive feel like they're going to die. I am one of them; gas mask over my face and nothing to do but wait, wait until my time comes.

Heather Blair (13)
Largs Academy, Largs

The Bag

I was waiting for my train. Someone had left a black leather bag. It moved. Something was inside. I opened it, curious. What was inside scared me, I could barely move. It jumped up and bit a woman walking by. She screamed. She went crazy and began biting and chasing everyone. The monkey was chewing someone's arm. In no time, I was the only one left that hadn't been bitten. It all happened so fast. I couldn't do anything! Everyone had been bitten. I sat slouched in the corner, watching. I turned away for one second and... it bit me.

Aimee Paterson-Caddell (14)
Largs Academy, Largs

The Nuclear Radiation Disaster

A nuclear disaster has occurred and there is smoke in the air. It smells of death. There are people's skeletons everywhere, but I am the only one who survived. It's quite scary and frightening that there is no one else but me! I can hear my Geiger counter going berserk and beeping. I can't touch anything but I keep forgetting to *not* touch things. I walk around safely. I forget not to touch something! I stop and fall over and that is it. I am gone, my heart stops beating and I will become a skeleton soon. Goodbye world.

Mathieu J Terry (13)
Largs Academy, Largs

Half The Battle

The science experiment went horribly and failed, causing mass chaos and destruction. Sam barely made it out of there. He was the only one still alive from the science lab. He ran as far away as he could, but now it was everywhere and he couldn't escape! He felt like he was getting smaller and smaller the more he looked around. Then he smelled the most horrible thing he had ever smelled, it was like a war zone from World War II. Frightened, scared, worried about what would happen next, he went as far away as he could from civilisation.

Josh Douglas Hill (12)
Largs Academy, Largs

Do Not Breathe!

I only took one breath. But that's all you need to take. One breath can give you the disease. All of humanity will end in less than a week. It's in the air. It's already wiped out half of the globe. It enters your brain and adds another type of consciousness. It enters your thoughts, persuades you to do things. You are persuaded to harm yourself and others. The human race is nearly over. Only two countries still have life in them. It persuades you to breathe on others, giving them the disease. It makes you kill other people.

Ryan Masterman (13)

Largs Academy, Largs

The Last Survivor

There was breaking news of a science experiment gone wrong that would affect all in existence. The day of the outbreak was nearly my last. Everyone was told to stay inside, to lock the windows and doors. I remember looking out of the window and seeing a swarm of green smoke raging its way through the town, destroying everything in its path.
Now I sit here alone, still locked up and away from humanity. The rest are dead, killed by the disease. The air is still polluted so I can't go outside. Soon I will starve to death and die.

Sarah Convery (12)
Largs Academy, Largs

The Eye Of The Last Survivor

The ground was shaking, we thought it was an earthquake but it was the undiscovered volcano of Everest. It let out a cloud of toxic gas. Everyone died, even my family. I'm the only survivor. I was confused and said, "Why me?"

Even my dog died. The skin on the bodies was rotting away. I needed to know why I was the only survivor, but there was something else. I saw a strange shadow coming closer and closer. A human! But it was holding something. I realised straight away it was a gun. He must have seen me. He fired.

Kris Ferguson (12)
Largs Academy, Largs

A River Of Red

Everything was great, except for the fact that some people were dead and the rest were bleeding through their eyes and mouths because of a disease made by the human race, designed to wipe out the human race, except for a select few that had been vaccinated just because they had blonde hair and blue eyes!
This Hitler guy in charge was just plain rude, thinking there was a 'supreme' race. What about all these people doing vital things for the human race? Just left to puke blood onto the street? 1946 is actually rubbish.

Callan McKee (13)
Largs Academy, Largs

It's Here

Crawling, burning, destroying. It had got to the last safe place. We were dead. Trapped like rats. Suddenly, it got through. How? The walls were pure steel. They had kept it out for months. As we ran out of the last safe place, we saw hundreds of bodies shrivelled up from the bite of that beast. But it was too fast, it caught us. Pinned us down. I escaped but my friend wasn't so lucky. I saw her lying on the ground, arm reaching out, moaning, crying for help. I'm safe now, but I'm not going to survive. It's here...

Anya Clare Milligan (12)
Largs Academy, Largs

Sunlight And Stealer

The land has become a freezing labyrinth of trunks and roots. The only way to escape the frozen hell is the fresh, burning lava of the Galapagos. The word tundra (meaning treeless) is now useless. Even the oceans are filled with towering mammoth trees from unknown lands. The trees sprouted up overnight. There were leaves covering all of the sky and absorbing the sunlight. Without the sun's light, the world froze over. The last humans remaining will soon perish without food.
Fineas Herbson, Botanist. 23/06/21.

Archie Scollin (12)
Largs Academy, Largs

The Pox

As the Arctic Disease Centre doors open, the ground trembles and all the lights smash. Out runs a man, trembling in fear as he collapses to the cold, icy ground, dead, bleeding everywhere. A rescue team comes and retrieves the corpse. The rescue team heads to America, but the team comes down with strange spots and dies. Suddenly, the whole of America is infected. The survivors work out the disease is a form of smallpox and realise the cure is all long gone. All they can do is sit back and wait for the inevitable end!

Brodie Donaldson (12)
Largs Academy, Largs

Abandoned

We snuck into the abandoned science lab. The lights didn't work so we used our phone torches. There were glass columns from floor to ceiling. My friend hit one of them with a bat and it smashed easily. Toxic gas started coming out of it. I covered my mouth and ran for the exit. My friend's eyes were glowing a pale red. He turned towards me and started following me. I ran down the corridor. I heard him breaking the other columns. I felt the gas burning my skin and making my eyes water. I hit a dead end...

Scarlett Macnamara (12)

Largs Academy, Largs

Killer Kidnapper

On a Friday, a little girl was having a birthday party. Her mum ordered a clown. About two hours later, all the kids disappeared, and the clown had too. Later, the mum found out the clown was a kidnapper. She looked everywhere but couldn't find them. She started to panic.

The kids were locked up in a small, light room with acid air. If they breathed in, they would die. The mum searched his name on the Internet and found the place that they might be. When she finally found the kids they were all dead.

Keziah Elizabeth Reid (12)
Largs Academy, Largs

The End Of The World

We finally heard the claxon. It was safe to leave. We emerged out of the bunker... slience. Everything was gone. The world was dying and we couldn't do anything about it. All around was quiet and eerie. The land was destroyed and there was no sign of life. We were shocked by how bad the war had been. One year and seventeen days underground and we seemed to be the only people who survived in our town. It was devastating to see our country, town and friends in the state that it had been turned into now.

Lauren Turner (13)
Largs Academy, Largs

Revenge Of The Zombola

One day, there was a mad scientist who created a disease that was made so he could control the world. He put it in the water supply and half the human race drank the water. Soon the world was in pieces and there were only 1000 humans alive. In a matter of hours, there were only 10 humans alive. Then every one of the zombies suddenly starting to die off.

A man called Devon was in a house with his family and was surprised to be alive. His wife and kids were traumatised at the sight of the dead bodies.

Lee Adams (13)
Largs Academy, Largs

When The Smog Comes

The fog horns were blowing, the people were screaming and all I could do was hold my breath and run. Already, half the world was contaminated by the deadly fog. Scientists were trying to figure out how to stop the fog. Maybe get a huge gust of wind to blow it away or maybe cover the town with some material so that the fog can't get in. But it was too late. The fog had already spread across the town. Now all we could do was say goodbye to all our loved ones and wait for our deaths to come.

Victoria Eve Murdoch (13)

Largs Academy, Largs

The Accident

Calum, Jamie and John were on the beach, skimming rocks. There was a road directly behind them. When they heard the blare of a horn, the boys looked behind them. An oil tanker landed right beside them with a leak in the tank. The boys screamed for help because the man driving the truck had died and the oil was contaminating the water, causing the fish to swim away. The boys stood there, thinking they needed to do something and they quit moaning and put a rock in the hole to stop the leak.

Robbie Woods (12)
Largs Academy, Largs

Immune

I looked up from the ashes and rubble. There was a thick fog and I could barely see a couple of feet in front of me. I felt my limbs to make sure they were still there and yelled to see if there were any other survivors, but there were none. My neck hurt and my legs were covered in scratches. Then I began to remember what happened. We were on a mission to end humanity. I was supposed to set off the bomb, the gases would burn out the lungs of every person on the planet. I was immune.

Ellise Fitzgerald (14)

Largs Academy, Largs

The Last Survivor Was Dead

It started as a little infection but it grew and grew. I was the only known survivor. My mum died, my brother too. Now it's coming for me. I ran out of food and water. I was stuck with nothing and no one. The water was contaminated. I knew I was going to be finished soon. I had lost my sight and hearing but I stood up and ran. But they were slowly crawling up me and biting me at the same time. I was weak. I could go no longer and I gave in. The last survivor was dead!

Emma McLarty (12)
Largs Academy, Largs

Last Man Standing

I was the last person on Earth, at least, I thought that. A virus was being analysed in a lab when it escaped through a hole in a glove. That's where it all started. It took my whole family, ate them from the inside out. Dead bodies littered the streets like plastic bags. I survived only on beans and Spam. It was my way of survival for the moment. I was about to fall asleep. I thought maybe it was my time, maybe I should just give up, maybe I should let them win?

Laurie Smith (12)
Largs Academy, Largs

The New Earth

When it came, I was one of the research professors who didn't get consumed but I wasn't untouched. It had run from professor to professor, devouring each one inside out. Its hunger was infinite. When it had finished devouring everyone else, it chased me. I was at the car when it leapt on me. It bit down and when it bit, I shrugged it off and drove to safety. Ever since then, I've had to vaccinate my leg to prevent the death that came with being bitten.

John Wilson (12)
Largs Academy, Largs

They're Gone

What's happened? Why is it so quiet? Cold, it's freezing like the sun has given up. There are people dead on the ground. They're blue and grey like someone dipped them in poison. I'm sprinting through the dead, cold people, trying to find someone alive. There's no one. I've found my house. It's been broken into. My pets are gone, my family is gone. No one except for me is alive. They're all gone!

Caera Murray (12)
Largs Academy, Largs

The Science Experiment

Somewhere in America in a lab, a science experiment went wrong and spread a virus that started to slowly kill people. The government stayed inside and didn't do anything about it. People were begging to be let inside but the government refused. A few days later, they ran out of food and it was super deadly outside. They couldn't go outside but they would starve. No one would survive this virus to make a cure...

Ruby Wilson (12)
Largs Academy, Largs

Man Vs Bear Trap

One day, there was a guy called Jacob. He woke up and saw people dying. He ran. They were being killed by zombies. He found a house. It was very modern and he saw a kid called Jay but he was stuck in a cupboard. So Jacob fly-kicked one zombie out of the window and saved him. He and Jay went into the barn. They saw something move so they both ran. Jacob got his foot caught in a bear trap and was about to get bitten...

James Harrison (12)
Largs Academy, Largs

Just The Two Of Us

At last, we came out of the basement that we had been in for 27 days. There was nobody, just the two of us, walking about, wondering why it was just us left. We were looking for people but there was nobody in sight. No food, no water, there was nothing. It was the end. There was nothing we could do.

Mia Caldwell Stevenson (12)
Largs Academy, Largs

Volatile

"Test Subject A is unaccounted for!"

"Where is Doctor Watson?"

"Sir, Doctor Watson's DNA, it's mutating!"

"What do you mean?"

"I mean he's turning into a Volatile!"

"But how did it infect him?"

"Sir, Test Subject A has gone but has left Doctor Watson mutating."

"We need to get out of here!"

Running down the hall, I witnessed everyone turning into a Volatile. Myself and Doctor Watson ran down the stairs with Test Subject A right behind us...

Three years later, we found refuge in an abandoned military base with a few others and we stayed there until the invasion...

Logan Peden (12)

Levenmouth Academy, Buckhaven

Soulless

We finally emerged from the underground bunker, gas masks clamped around our faces. I wasn't fazed by the corpses that greeted us as we were already well acquainted with them, thanks to the daily broadcasts on television. I was, however, shocked by the scarlet rashes that covered their bodies and the soulless expressions on their faces - those little 'unimportant' details weren't captured. The air was chilled from the lack of human presence. We advanced towards the truck, trampling over the bodies, mothers and brothers and friends. We piled in upon reaching the truck and sped away to save human civilisation.

Leah Nisbet (14)
Levenmouth Academy, Buckhaven

Invasion

The first thing that came into my head was, *run*, but my legs wouldn't move. About 1,000,000 bugs were coming my way and as they almost hit my legs, someone came and pulled me away. Still in shock, we arrived at this small cave where there were lots of families sitting close together. Their faces were filled with fear. A tall man with long, black hair and a long, curly beard shouted, "That's them all!"

A big boulder sealed the opening.

"No one gets in or out."

But it doesn't matter, we're all going to die of hunger someday...

Alyx Winn (12)
Levenmouth Academy, Buckhaven

The Infectious Outdoors

Scientists were all to blame for this apocalyptic fate. That incident at the lab where the dangerous chemicals were released into the air has changed the world forever. Now I resided in an underground base, which will never be like home. It was the only safe place though. Outside, victims inhaled that toxic mix and suffered the devastating consequences. Now, millions lay in this bed of poison, lifeless. I stepped further down this dull tunnel when I suddenly saw light. This area was home to an opening... Contaminated air greeted me. I faced the infectious outdoors...

Emma Louise Roberts (15)
Levenmouth Academy, Buckhaven

Freeing The World

The last drop fell into the test tube, everyone crowding around it as it turned a deep shade of emerald. A feeling of relief fell across the room, they'd finally done it, they'd found the cure. The cure for nomophobia. The cure to rid the world from the zombies that inhabit it. Maybe now the world can go back to how it was before; before technology turned most of the population into the walking dead, living every moment of their lives with a little black box in their hand or back pocket. "Now we go back to curing real viruses."

Holly Tracy Wilson (17)
Levenmouth Academy, Buckhaven

The Infection

The disease was spreading rapidly, everybody was getting infected. Everywhere you looked, there were piles of dead bodies. There was no way out. Everyone was trapped. I felt a weird sensation on my arm, I looked down to see an insect scuttling on my arm. I quickly pinged it off but it was too late, I was already infected! I could feel my body warming up. An uncontrollable sweat broke out, I was itching like crazy! Skin started to peel off, clumps of hair began to fall out, red lumps formed all over my body. I was dead within seconds!

Aymen Rao Rizwan (13)
Levenmouth Academy, Buckhaven

Children Of The Apocalypse

The five children sat in their boarded-up tree house with their pots and pan hats, one with his Swiss Army Knife, the rest with bats. They know they were the last people in their neighbourhood. One kid called Walter had an IQ upwards of 197. He was sitting, building a radio to try to get help out of the dome the zombies were contained in. The government knew they were still in there but told everyone there was no one there. Finally, the radio worked but it was a one-way channel. No one would hear them. They'd be stuck forever.

Joseph Wilson (12)
Levenmouth Academy, Buckhaven

Faceless

As I opened the door of the derelict building, a strong smell smacked me in the face, like hundreds of rocks. I started to step into the building. I looked down on the floor... there were bits of people's skin everywhere. As I got to the end room, there were bodies with their faces burned off. I heard a bang and the building shook. I ran outside and it was like I was in a world of my own, everyone's faces were all melted off. People and animals were dropping like flies. I said, "That's it, my life is over!"

Jason Yule (13)
Levenmouth Academy, Buckhaven

B235 Dilemma

Something banged on my door. I went to see what it was.

"Help! I'm turning into a zombie!"

I slammed the door shut and ran to the attic. Not realising the disease was airborne, I opened the window. I turn round and saw a box that had 'Take me to the government' written on it. I grabbed my keys and got in my car and drove to the government HQ. When I arrived, I said I had a package I needed to deliver. I was allowed through. The package was identified as B235, in other words, the cure.

Declan Ferrier (12)
Levenmouth Academy, Buckhaven

Run

The zombies were coming closer and closer. We had to run. Run 'til we found shelter.
It was two hours later and we'd found a hideout. We went in but we had to run back out again. There were zombies. They saw us and started coming after us so we tried to run, but two zombies had our legs. We couldn't move. We felt dizzy. I fell. My friend then fell too. He opened his eyes. They were red and he looked like he wanted to eat me. Then everything went black. My head hurt and I felt different...

Hollie Elizabeth Glenn McCulloch (12)
Levenmouth Academy, Buckhaven

The Survival

It was the day of survival. People were running around screaming, panicking and looking for medicine they needed, otherwise they would die. One nurse came along and said, "I know where the medicine you need is."
Everyone was lining up for some medicine. The nurse grabbed a needle and injected a clear liquid into their arms. One by one, people started shaking and hyperventilating. The nurse's injection was more poison! They all fell to the ground. Some lived, some died.

Jaimie Ann Thomson Walters (14)
Levenmouth Academy, Buckhaven

We Are Trapped

We are trapped. The world is contaminated...
People are dropping dead like dominoes. Everyone
in this little bunker are the last survivors. If we
leave, we die and if we stay, we starve. There is
literally no way of surviving this horror. I know the
cure is out there, but even if my pinkie goes
outside this bunker I'm dead! I've had enough of
sitting in this bunker. I want to find the cure, so I
leave the bunker. I almost reach the hopsital but
then the infection gets me...

Jasmin Scarlett (13)
Levenmouth Academy, Buckhaven

The Hydra

The world has been contaminated. There are only 850 to 950 people in this base or cage, or whatever you want to call it. We think we have found or made the first part of the cure and the government is locked down in a base somewhere else. A monster called The Hydra caused all of this, but you won't kill it. The only way is to inject it with the gas or whatever, but the only bad thing is that we have to get close and nobody wants to take that risk. We're in danger, help!

Tyler Wilson
Levenmouth Academy, Buckhaven

Matter Of Time

'Dear Diary,
It's been about two months since I have seen the outside world. The last thing I saw were my neighbours, the Williamses, get taken and eaten. Our food is slowly depleting. We stayed away from the water in the taps, we think it's spread through that. I can hear them scratching and banging their bodies against the doors and windows. They know that we are in here. It's just a matter of time.'

Dylan Keddie (13)
Levenmouth Academy, Buckhaven

Cure Gone Wrong

The screams... the fire... I remember the day my camp was destroyed. Intel didn't know what they were doing. A scientist was running down the corridor. That foolish man was my brother. He was calling out, "I've found it, I've found it!"
He just wanted to impress his boss. He'd found the cure for cancer or at least he thought he had. It was actually a zombie disease! I was in the military camp that day. The zombies destroyed it. The support came. They nuked the southern hemisphere, hoping it would get rid of them. It didn't...

Scott Stewart (13)
McLaren High School, Callander

Behind Me

"It's okay boy, it's me..."

Growl! The foul beast jumped up. My shotgun slipped out of my hand. I punched the beast, then grabbed the weapon and took a shot. The kick of the gun pushed me back. The spread of the cartridge pellets flew right to the foul beast's noggin, exploding his head right off his neck. The loud booming noise deafened me. Then more growling started. As it came closer and closer, the horde came too. I fired my last cartridge. The gun was empty. I ran to the pier. The horde was right behind me now...

Tom McCulloch (13)
McLaren High School, Callander

In The Bunker

The sounds of the world outside filled the lonely, still room where Max lay silently, observing the place where he'd lived for many months in fear of the world outside. As Max began to stir, he moved from his sleeping bag where he had lain in the bunker's four walls, trying to retain heat as the old military bunker had been forgotten about for years. He started the routine that he repeated every day. With the same feel of horror, he opened the door. *I believe I'm the only one left after the accident that happened*, he thought to himself...

Hannah Docherty (13)
McLaren High School, Callander

Medical Germ Facility Disaster

From the medical germ facility, a dangerous virus has got out and is threatening mankind as we know it. I always thought of it as some sort of joke but now it's real. I'm scared, confused. I don't know what to do. A search party is trying desperately to evacuate everyone in the area. I can't believe this is happening. I feel sick, I can't breathe. I drop slowly. I fall, screaming. I'm down. I can feel something on my skin. It bites me, ripping my skin. I wail out. It starts scuttling around and I take one final gasp.

Robert Tweedie
McLaren High School, Callander

Brains

This story starts not when I was a zombie but when I was just a young boy having fun playing Fortnite. Then, a scream. I shouted, "Mum, Dad!"
My mum and dad came running in and said, "Go!" So I ran, no, I sprinted away, wanting to look back but I couldn't bring myself to. I found a cave.
A week later, I left the cave. I went back to my house. I knocked, I waited, I entered. My dad? He was there but I had a strange urge. Then I put my hands out and walked forwards saying, "Brains..."

Benjamin Snow (13)

McLaren High School, Callander

It's Over

The giant, poisonous gas cloud rises into the skies, killing our animals, crashing our birds and poisoning the air so with every breath our lives are being risked more and more. I wake up and, for a second, forget where I am. What is this thing over my mouth and nose? Why am I rocking around? Where is Mother and Father and dear Maggie? It's all coming back now. I sit up and look at the world flying by outside the carriage. The only memory of home is my old backpack and my dog, Bailey. That's it, it's over...

Camryn Taylor Reynolds (12)
McLaren High School, Callander

The Deadly Infection

Something scuttled under my skin. I could feel the warmth of its scaly body getting hungry for my blood with every step. I was in need of help.

Soon I was at the hospital waiting in a queue. With my heartbeat thumping, I heard, "Freddy Waldo!" get shouted.

The very sound of my name made me leap. Slowly but surely, I entered the room. Hearing my footsteps echoing made it even worse.

Hours later, I left the room that I had entered.

As usual, the doctors had no words to explain my infection.

All they called it was a rash.

Codie McGowan (12)
Stewarton Academy, Stewarton

Fault In The System

The rash was spreading, pulsing, hurting. Natalie couldn't believe it. Sophie couldn't let this happen, it was terrible. Sophie looked over at Natalie in her hospital bed, close to tears. The dingy hospital ward didn't help when trying to keep spirits high. All the other Corpus patients had been cured. Why wasn't it working for Natalie? The cure would've been 100% successful if it wasn't for Natalie. There were doctors constantly fussing over her and she was always so tired...

Her mother cried as she stood over the casket. It was devastating news what'd happened to Natalie. Everyone was grieving.

Lara Haine (13)
Stewarton Academy, Stewarton

114

Rain

There was no bang, no boom and no explosion. But rather, there was rain and screaming... I look up and instantly recoil. The sharp sting I feel all over my body tells me immediately that something is wrong. The fluid now seeps through to my scalp, singeing my roots, causing the hair to fall from my head. We're all stumbling around blind, desperately seeking refuge. Soon enough, I give up and conclude it's useless. We're as good as dead. The screams are overwhelming. The pain, the fear, the screaming won't end. I'm done. I'm finished. Please make it stop...

Molly McDade (14)
Stewarton Academy, Stewarton

Breathe

29th of March. That's when it came. If you breathed, you died. A slow helpless process. Boils and blisters appeared, bursting with acid. Rashes, loss of mind. There was no hope for the weak. Nowhere was safe. Those who ran were engulfed by disease and death. Families were in graves, buildings were ashes. The gas still marched around the streets, smelling like everything you hated. Even the birds didn't chirp. No form of food, water, medicine. Everything contaminated. Oxygen masks were out. It was only a matter of time. Only the toughened survived.
So... where is everyone?

May McLaughlin (14)
Stewarton Academy, Stewarton

The Blood Genocide

It's the blood. I rip my skin apart, scratching, desperate to get the poison out. Everyone around me is the same, realising simultaneously that our blood has become toxic. My body aches as my blood literally boils. It stops spilling out of my cuts, solidifying! I feel myself stiffening. People press alarms, chaos spreads throughout the patients. Nobody comes. They've planned this - a genocide. They're killing us off! A million thoughts run through my head. My family, my daughter. Ironically, I was here to have my appendix removed to *stop* the pain. I'll never see my daughter grow up...

Teagan Neish (15)
Stewarton Academy, Stewarton

Five Foot Under

The giant, poisonous cloud rose into the sky.
"I never meant for this to happen..."
Fifty years later... Fifty years since I last had a breath of fresh air. I have been living underground all this time. There is only me left of the human race. Fifty years ago, a scientist made a serum that exploded into the sky and has caused eternal poisonous rain. If this rain touches me, I will burn to death. I am now in the middle of nowhere underground and I have almost run out of food and water. Help, I'm going to die...

Ellie Anderson (14)
Stewarton Academy, Stewarton

Hounds From Hell

The cure had to be here somewhere, the thing that would destroy the inexorable predator of the human race once known as man's best friend. I frantically scavenged through the endless amount of paper on Dr Hutner's desk, hopelessly trying to find something that would save me from the pack of demonic hounds scratching behind the barricaded door. The idea was to create a form of war dog that could protect soldiers from danger, but all it did was create a virus that changed our beloved pets forever. Now they were man's greatest threat. Suddenly, the barricade broke...

Johanna-Ellie Robertson (14)
Stewarton Academy, Stewarton

A New Discovery?

As the last drop fell into the test tube, my heart was pounding. Had I done it? Had I, a silly scientist, discovered a cure for this apocalypse?

"All I need to do now is test it," I muttered under my breath.

But how? I thought. *Zombies are everywhere!* My mind went blank. What was I to do? *I know! The army and explorers are outside the bunker, they can help spread the antidote.* I scrambled outside with my heart in my stomach; this was the moment. Jumping onto the helicopter with the antidote in hand, I poured it. *Boom...*

Louise Macaulay (13)
Stewarton Academy, Stewarton

Outbreak

It was spreading, pulsing, hurting. Earlier, I'd found my parents lying on the floor, convulsing. I panicked, locked them in the kitchen and locked myself in the bathroom. I was in shock and confusion. *Where are the answers to my problems?* I thought to myself. *Twitter!* My feed was filled with people looking for answers but nobody knew the causes of it. I read an article on the rates at which people were turning into these creatures. It was too much so I washed my face to calm myself. That's when it started, the spreading, pulsing and hurting...

Blake Hannah (14)
Stewarton Academy, Stewarton

Three Days, One Chance

It's scary when you're told the world will end in three days but when you are one of the very people that everyone's relying on to fix it, it's much worse. I only had one chance. The cancer cure was a breakthrough. However, the gas-based supposed miracle drug spread everywhere and did damage way beyond anyone's control, not only destroying cancer cells, but taking every living being and thing too. When everyone in the world has gone, you're left by yourself with only the words *you had one chance* playing on a loop in your head...

Madeline Esther McIlreavy (14)
Stewarton Academy, Stewarton

Beginning Of The End

We finally emerged from the underground bunker. The usual fields of green and coloured flowers had been transformed into a misty, dark land. No sun. The plants had shrivelled to a crisp. Within only a couple of minutes, we realised what had happened and quickly scrambled to attach our gas masks in time. We were stunned more than anything. The threat of nuclear war had come true. America had done it. Our home, Israel, had been turned into a scene from the apocalypse. I realised the extent of what'd happened when I looked at the hole dissolving in my foot...

Jamie Mitchell (14)
Stewarton Academy, Stewarton

Who's Next?

The human race has contracted a disease. Everyone I know is falling down around me. It is almost like something out of a book or a movie. The government is killing their own people. They've let us down. That one test subject soon became two, then three, then four, then hundreds, now millions. I've watched my own family drown in a sea of lifeless bodies. It's not even like I can leave here, I've got nowhere to go. The infected just keep multiplying. We, the uninfected, just seem to keep losing more by the day. No one knows who's next...

Christopher Lennon (14)
Stewarton Academy, Stewarton

The Scientist

The alarm was blaring. Screams tore through my ears. Footsteps pounded on the laminate flooring. I picked up one of the many injection needles scattered around my feet. The oddly green-coloured liquid was bubbling excitedly inside the tube. Thin particles of dust surrounded me, floating around my head. I noticed the man with the white lab coat lying crumpled in the corner against a wall. His breathing was abnormal. Lumps were bubbling up on his hands, spreading up his arms. I knelt down beside him. His eyes shot open widely. Blood red was their colour...

Emily Smith (14)
Stewarton Academy, Stewarton

The Rise Of The Poisonous Cloud

We finally emerged from the underground bunker into the hazardous wasteland. We were the first living humans to step out into the wasteland for thirty years. Our first thought when we were attacked by unknown creatures, who had with them a poisonous cloud which could easily destroy the human race, was would we ever see our planet again? When this happened, we were the only people who didn't die as we had a specialised underground bunker which the poison could not reach. This poison was still active now but we needed to erase it. Would we live or die?

Alexander Caulfield (14)
Stewarton Academy, Stewarton

No More Earth

The giant, poisonous cloud rose into the sky, shooting poison lightning. People were running everywhere and dying with the poison. Scientists were working day and night, trying to save the world. One little kid wanted to save the world but she didn't know how.

A few days later, she had it - she would fly some people to Mars! She set to work but building a rocket and chose who was going on the rocket. She got the rocket and set it on its way. But, on the way there, the poisonous cloud came out of nowhere and ate it!

Catriona Muir (12)
Stewarton Academy, Stewarton

The Dr

The last drop fell into the test tube. The scientist sitting in the chair at his work station grinned, pleased that he had cured humanity and could fix the ravaged world outside his decaying laboratory in a large forest somewhere in the UK. Now, he needed to distribute the cure to sanitary locations the government had established around the country. The only problem was he was the only non-addicted human within miles. He had to go. Growls and wails came from the infected horde, waiting for the old doctor ro set off into the apocalyptic woodland...

Faris Marshall (14)
Stewarton Academy, Stewarton

The Lights

I had everything before the lights. That's what they're calling them. Theories are flying around but one thing's for certain, people are dying and fast. My life was so perfect, I had everything, the perfect job, the perfect family. Then two days ago, I watched them die. It all started with the lights, like the clouds were on fire. Then everyone started dying for no apparent reason. My beautiful two-year-old daughter, gone. A group of us are hiding but with few supplies. I can't help but think something unimaginable is coming...

Rebecca Smith (14)
Stewarton Academy, Stewarton

Pandora's Plague

We finally emerged from the bunker. The air stank of rot. I could feel the death lurking, mingling with my senses. All of a sudden, my mind wandered back. I saw the school, my friends, the days when life was bliss. That day was just as normal... until the plague hit. I'd rushed to the janitor's closet, thinking it would be safe. I ended up blacking out. The plague was one of God's send outs, another opening of Pandora's box. It caused a leak in the pipe of humanity, a dysfunctional, apocalyptic Earth. Time to find the cure...

Max McCaughran (13)
Stewarton Academy, Stewarton

The Walter Brothers

J and M Walter, the two richest men in the world, the biggest manufacturers of medical needles. Ever had a jab? It was one of their needles. You were probably sick at the time, something the Walter brothers didn't agree with. In their eyes, all the sick should be wiped out and so they started to put traces of poison in every needle. Within days people died, before we knew it, billions had died and nobody could figure out why. How could a harmless infection kill someone? The horrifying truth hit me when I felt the prick in my arm...

Jane Docherty McDowell (15)
Stewarton Academy, Stewarton

The Mistake

As I switched on the TV, guilt overtook me. Everyone was dropping dead. It was all my fault. You see, I used to be a scientist, now I was a mass murderer. All I wanted to do was cure cancer. I didn't think my cure would become an airborne disease started by a rat coming into my lab. I didn't even know my serum was incorrect. I didn't mean it, I really didn't. The damage had been done now. I couldn't think of a way to reverse it. I was one of the only ones uninfected in Washington. "I'm sorry."

Adam Nadeem (15)
Stewarton Academy, Stewarton

The Attack

I was asleep when they attacked. They must have been infected recently because they still looked human except for their pitch-black eyes. They attacked like animals. No one knew how it started but it was spreading fast with no sign of stopping. Only four of us survived the initial attack. I thought I was in the clear until I saw blood dripping from the scratch. I prayed it wasn't from their fingernails. If it was, I would have about half a minute left. Now there were two choices - I could end my own life or I could join them...

Emma Nimmo (14)
Stewarton Academy, Stewarton

The Bomb Shelter

We finally emerged into the underground bunker, saving us from the radioactive bomb that could have blown us into one million bits. We knew we weren't totally safe but it was good we were all in the bunker. Our main concern was food and water, but we all knew we would be dead in a second if we went into the toxic wasteland without a gas mask. The reader who's reading this is probably wondering what happened before. Let me tell you. First, it was the blazing sirens, then it was the running. It was terrifying for everyone...

Peter A Millar (12)
Stewarton Academy, Stewarton

The Breakout

The last drop fell into the test tube as the door pounded open. They were coming fast. Carter sprinted down the narrow road, making sure no zombies were in sight. He was going to the hospital to check on his newborn baby sister, Ella. She had just been born when the breakout happened. As he approached the door, he opened it with caution. All he wanted to do was save her. Finally, as he approached the ward, he could hear them coming up the stairs. Carter saw his sister, still and groaning. She was green. She had been turned...

Niamh Russell (12)
Stewarton Academy, Stewarton

Last Breath

The giant, poisonous cloud rose into the sky as Gas Lurker finished off a group of survivors by choking them with a gas grenade. They screamed with pain as their eyes started to bleed and lungs burned. From a distance, Gas Lurker spotted a sealed-off house. He crept over, unholstered his LMG, blasted the sealed door off and left a gas trap for the people in the house to die. Eighteen survivors tried to run. They had no chance. He enjoyed seeing his victims suffer and he would never forget the horrific beauty he'd created.

Malcolm Millar (12)
Stewarton Academy, Stewarton

Underneath

We finally emerged from the underground bunker, the sun beaming down on us (me and James that is). We'd been in that bunker since the day it happened, the day the animals turned on humans. We were lucky, me and James, we were both on watch duty, checking for any survivors of the Safara War. It was dusk when we saw a cheetah charge at us, somehow spotting us from inside our camouflaged base. Animals usually left us alone but not now. I pounced upon my shotgun. The cheetah now at the base, I shot and the cheetah was dead...

Rhuaridh Longstaff (12)
Stewarton Academy, Stewarton

The Mass Revenge

We've finally emerged from the underground bunker me and Boyd have been hiding in for over six months. There are terrible things happening to our world right now, or should I say *their* world! They are the aliens, or that's what we call them. Right now, it is 2225. The aliens came in 2200. One of their ships crash-landed in 2200 but there were only 250 on board. The army finished them all off but one. He went back and got everyone from his planet which turned out to be over 10,000,000! The ships came, full...

Nathan Lamont McDowell (12)
Stewarton Academy, Stewarton

Saviour

I wander through the valley, shrouded in shadows and death. yet I fear not the evil that may come for me, from my own mind. I may be broken, fragmented, shattered but I know I'll face my demons when they come for me. Everyone else did, their minds in tatters, left to destroy themselves from the inside out. I come upon a man at the top of a hill. He calls himself the savour of the human race. He says he's come to save the world from destruction and pain. I say, "How can you save the world from itself?"

Zara Elizabeth Conroy-Rodger (14)
Stewarton Academy, Stewarton

Silence

As the chemicals reached his brain, all the characteristics of my brother disappeared. The goofy smile I knew so well was consumed by the pain. I held his shaking hand as the pain in his eyes grew, growing until there was nothing left. I stood and took one last look at the empty world. If only we had had more time. There was so much I hadn't done. I looked down at my brother as the pain started. Lying next to him, I let it take over, taking over everything until there was nothing left. And then there was silence.

Eilidh Allan (14)
Stewarton Academy, Stewarton

Tagged

"It's okay, it's me, Mum."
I turned the handle hesitantly and opened the door. Her eyes were jet-black. Immediately, I smelt death. She had been tagged. She stretched her ghostly hands out to grab me but I bolted. I spotted the front door from the top of the stairs. I turned and saw my mum chasing me. My blood ran cold. I jumped from the top stair to the bottom. My hand grasped the handle and I turned it to find out I was locked in. It was too late. I was tagged...

Josslyn Fletcher (14)
Stewarton Academy, Stewarton

The Cloud

The giant, poisonous cloud rose into the sky. I was in the park alone but content and happy. I was on my way home from my friend's house when I saw it - the huge, green, stinking, poisonous cloud of lethal gas that could kill you within two minutes of inhaling just the smallest breath. I looked around but there was nothing, so my only options were to die or to take my jumper off and cover my nose and mouth. I ran and didn't stop but I fell, landing on a rock. I was lying on the ground, bleeding...

Kyle Maitland (12)
Stewarton Academy, Stewarton

Could Have Gone Better

The last drop fell into the test tube. Suddenly, there was a strange smell in the air. Nobody could quite put their finger on it but we all knew that we hated it. I turned around and I saw that there was a puff of green smoke coming out of the test tube. In the blink of an eye, the smoke was all around the room. Bodies were dropping to the floor all around me. I did not know what to do! I managed to escape the room but I later realised that I'd left the door wide open...

Cara Moffat (12)
Stewarton Academy, Stewarton

The Virus

"Test subject A is unaccounted for," announced a robot. "Should we abort?"
"No," replied a woman's voice lazily from a chair. "Continue test." The robot flipped a switch and six pods began to glow, five with humans inside. In three months, a virus would kill most of the world's population. No one would know someone was responsible. They would think it was an accident but really, Doctor Sanders would be responsible. Right now, subject A, or Alex, was in the shadows. A knife glinted. She wouldn't, she couldn't let them ruin the world. Doctor Sanders suddenly spoke icily. "Hello Alex..."

Isla Webb (12)
Webster's High School, Kirriemuir

Patient Zero - Hell's Worst Epidemic

"Find her, now!"

The girl grinned above them. Stupid things. Scuttling quickly, vent lifting, she dropped. It didn't even have time to scream, let alone get its gun. Her blood sang but no victory, not yet, she couldn't make a sound. Her wings fluttered, faster than a hummingbird's, faster than light. The head scientist couldn't be far. All she had to do was find him... and end him, not mercifully and quickly like the others. He'd torn her open, carved her up. She heard them - footsteps. Her fangs dripped red. She grinned, hungry, a gaping chasm sensing him...

Cassandra Calder (16)

Webster's High School, Kirriemuir

Run

"Run!" he screamed. And I did. My legs burned with pain with every step. The branches ripped my skin as I ran further into the woods, not looking back. The branches came at me like daggers. What hurt most was the growing pain in my arm, slowly feeding into my fingertips, a tingling feeling. My whole body felt paralysed, everything except my thoughts, eyeballs and ears. Then I heard the voice coming from behind, "Oh my God, I've found you! I thought it'd got you."
My mind started to blur. Only one thought was in my head now - *kill*...

Cora East
Webster's High School, Kirriemuir

The Creature

Slowly he opened the rusting door and stepped into the grimy room. There was a light but nobody could remember the last time it'd worked. He carried on into the pod room and tapped the panel, releasing one of them. He tried to remember his training, that they weren't human, at least not anymore. Before it could do anything, Iven instantly tasered it till unconscious. Even through his mask, he could smell the putrefaction. A faint sucking sound came as it slowly slid to the floor. Carrying it to the workbench, he saw his bloodstained scalpel. Suddenly, the creature moved...

Rory Fyles (13)
Webster's High School, Kirriemuir

Ventilation

The ventilator hummed quietly and the green light flashed, assuring her that it was keeping the air inside clean. Outside her window, the infected lay on the pavement, waiting for death to free them from their pain. Not a single doctor would attempt to save them; it was suicide to step outside. She refreshed her social media for what seemed like the hundredth time, but it returned blank. The Internet was down. She sighed. For just a moment, it was silent. Too silent. She looked at the ventilator. A red light was flashing.
An urgent notification pinged onto the screen.

Alix Burness (15)
Webster's High School, Kirriemuir

The Bugs From Hell

"The bugs fly around with no care in the world, eating, killing, destroying. You don't know you're on your deathbed until you feel one crawling under your skin. They inject poison into your veins and lay eggs in your body. The poison strikes your heart within a minute, turning your skin blue and making you ice-cold. Your eyes go red and your skin starts to crack, turning you into a jigsaw."

Hearing those words from the doctor made me feel sick. My mother was dead like so many others. Then I felt a tingle under my skin...

Ellie Craib (12)
Webster's High School, Kirriemuir

Am I?

It's been a few days now. Am I almost a zombie? There's an infection on my arm. I feel terrible about not telling my friend. We were at a little house in the middle of nowhere. I woke up that morning. I went to the mirror. My skin was green! Now, it'll be only a few hours before the behaviour kicks in. I can't go see my friend like this as they would kill me. Or would it be better if I let them kill me? Or should I... should I... kill them? And if so, who first?

Anna Goubet (14)
Webster's High School, Kirriemuir

YOUNG WRITERS INFORMATION

We hope you have enjoyed reading this book – and that you will continue to in the coming years.

If you're a young writer who enjoys reading and creative writing, or the parent of an enthusiastic poet or story writer, do visit our website **www.youngwriters.co.uk**. Here you will find free competitions, workshops and games, as well as recommended reads, a poetry glossary and our blog.

If you would like to order further copies of this book, or any of our other titles, then please give us a call or order via your online account.

Young Writers
Remus House
Coltsfoot Drive
Peterborough
PE2 9BF
(01733) 890066
info@youngwriters.co.uk

Join in the conversation!

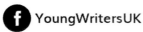 YoungWritersUK   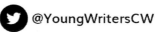 @YoungWritersCW